melville house classics

A SLEEP
AND A
FORGETTING

A SLEEP AND A FORGETTING

WILLIAM DEAN HOWELLS

MELVILLE HOUSE PUBLISHING
BROOKLYN, NEW YORK

A SLEEP AND A FORGETTING FIRST APPEARED IN THE COLLECTION
BETWEEN THE DARK AND THE DAYLIGHT: ROMANCES IN 1907.

BOOK DESIGN: DAVID KONOPKA

MELVILLE HOUSE PUBLISHING
145 PLYMOUTH STREET
BROOKLYN, NY 11201

WWW.MHPBOOKS.COM

ISBN 13: 978-0-9766583-8-2

FIRST MELVILLE HOUSE PRINTING: MAY 2009

LIBRARY OF CONGRESS CATALOGING-IN-PUBLICATION DATA

HOWELLS, WILLIAM DEAN, 1837-1920.
 A SLEEP AND A FORGETTING / WILLIAM DEAN HOWELLS.
   P. CM. --(THE ART OF THE NOVELLA)
  ISBN-13: 978-0-9766583-8-2 (AL. PAPER)
  ISBN-10: 0-9766583-8-0 (ALK. PAPER)
1. PHYSICIANS--FICTION. 2. YOUNG WOMEN--FICTION.
3. AMNESIACS--FICTION. 4. PSYCHOLOGICAL FICTION.
I. TITLE. II. SERIES.
 PS2029.S64 2006
 813.4--DC22

                          2006012774

A SLEEP AND A FORGETTING

Matthew Lanfear had stopped off, between Genoa and Nice, at San Remo in the interest of a friend who had come over on the steamer with him, and who wished him to test the air before settling there for the winter with an invalid wife. She was one of those neurasthenics who really carry their climate—always a bad one—with them, but she had set her mind on San Remo; and Lanfear was willing to pass a few days in the place making the observations which he felt pretty sure would be adverse.

His train was rather late, and the sunset was fading from the French sky beyond the Italian shore when he got out of his car and looked round for a porter to take his valise. His roving eye lighted on the anxious figure, which as fully as the anxious face, of a short, stout, elderly man expressed a sort of distraction, as he stood loaded down with umbrellas, bags, bundles, and wraps, and seemed unable to arrest the movements of a tall young girl, with a travelling-shawl trailing from her arm, who had the effect of escaping from him towards a bench beside the door of the waiting-room. When she reached it, in spite of his appeals, she sat down with an absent air, and looked as far withdrawn from the bustle of the platform and from the snuffling train as if on some quiet garden seat along with her own thoughts.

In his fat frenzy, which Lanfear felt to be pathetic, the old gentleman glanced at him, and then abruptly demanded: "Are you an American?"

They knew each other abroad in some mystical way, and Lanfear did not try to deny the fact.

"Oh, well, then," the stranger said, as if the fact made everything right, "will you kindly tell my daughter, on that bench by the door yonder"—he pointed with a bag, and dropped a roll of rugs from under his arm—"that I'll be with her as soon as I've looked after the trunks? Tell her not to move till I come. Heigh! Here! Take hold of these, will you?" He caught the sleeve of a *facchino* who came wandering by, and heaped him with his burdens, and then pushed ahead of the man in the direction of the baggage-room with a sort of mastery of the situation which struck Lanfear as springing from desperation rather than experience.

Lanfear stood a moment hesitating. Then a glance

at the girl on the bench, drooping a little forward in freeing her face from the veil that hung from her pretty hat, together with a sense of something quaintly charming in the confidence shown him on such purely compatriotic grounds, decided him to do just what he had been asked. The girl had got her veil up by this time, and as he came near, she turned from looking at the sunset over the stretch of wall beyond the halting train, and met his dubious face with a smile.

"It *is* beautiful, isn't it?" she said. "I know I shall get well, here, if they have such sunsets every day."

There was something so convincingly normal in her expression that Lanfear dismissed a painful conjecture. "I beg your pardon," he said. "I am afraid there's some mistake. I haven't the pleasure—You must excuse me, but your father wished me to ask you to wait here for him till he had got his baggage—"

"My father?" the girl stopped him with a sort of a frowning perplexity in the stare she gave him. "My father isn't here!"

"I beg your pardon," Lanfear said. "I must have misunderstood. A gentleman who got out of the train with you—a short, stout gentleman with gray hair—I understood him to say you were his daughter—requested me to bring this message—"

The girl shook her head. "I don't know him. It must be a mistake."

"The mistake is mine, no doubt. It may have been some one else whom he pointed out, and I have blundered. I'm very sorry if I seem to have intruded—"

"What place is this?" the girl asked, without noticing his excuses.

"San Remo," Lanfear answered. "If you didn't intend to stop here, your train will be leaving in a moment."

"I meant to get off, I suppose," she said. "I don't believe I'm going any farther." She leaned back against the bars of the bench, and put up one of her slim arms along the top.

There was something wrong. Lanfear now felt that, in spite of her perfect tranquillity and self-possession; perhaps because of it. He had no business to stay there talking with her, but he had not quite the right to leave her, though practically he had got his dismissal, and apparently she was quite capable of taking care of herself, or could have been so in a country where any woman's defencelessness was not any man's advantage. He could not go away without some effort to be of use.

"I beg your pardon," he said. "Can I help you in calling a carriage; or looking after your hand-baggage—it will be getting dark—perhaps your maid—"

"My *maid*!" The girl frowned again, with a measure of the amazement which she showed when he mentioned her father. "*I* have no maid!"

Lanfear blurted desperately out: "You are alone? You came—you are going to stay here—alone?"

"Quite alone," she said, with a passivity in which there was no resentment, and no feeling unless it were a certain color of dignity. Almost at the same time, with a glance beside and beyond him, she called out joyfully: "Ah, there you are!" and Lanfear turned, and saw scuffling and heard puffing towards them the short, stout elderly gentleman who had sent him to her. "I knew you would come before long!"

"Well, I thought it was pretty long, myself," the gentleman said, and then he courteously referred himself to Lanfear. "I'm afraid this gentleman has found it rather long, too; but I couldn't manage it a moment sooner."

Lanfear said: "Not at all. I wish I could have been of any use to—"

"My daughter—Miss Gerald, Mr.—"

"Lanfear—Dr. Lanfear," he said, accepting the introduction; and the girl bowed.

"Oh, doctor, eh?" the father said, with a certain impression. "Going to stop here?"

"A few days," Lanfear answered, making way for the forward movement which the others began.

"Well, well! I'm very much obliged to you, very much, indeed; and I'm sure my daughter is."

The girl said, "Oh yes, indeed," rather indifferently, and then as they passed him, while he stood lifting his hat, she turned radiantly on him. "Thank you, ever so much!" she said, with the gentle voice which he had already thought charming.

The father called back: "I hope we shall meet again. We are going to the Sardegna."

Lanfear had been going to the Sardegna himself, but while he bowed he now decided upon another hotel.

The mystery, whatever it was, that the brave, little, fat father was carrying off so bluffly, had clearly the morbid quality of unhealth in it, and Lanfear could not give himself freely to a young pleasure in the girl's dark beauty of eyes and hair, her pale, irregular, piquant face, her slender figure and flowing walk. He was in the presence of something else, something that appealed to his scientific side, to that which was humane more than that which was human in him, and abashed him in the other feeling. Unless she was out of her mind there was no way of accounting for her behavior, except by some caprice which was itself scarcely short of insanity. She must have thought she knew him when he approached, and when she addressed him those first words; but when he had tried to set her right she had not changed; and why had she denied her father, and then hailed him with joy when he came back to her? She had known that she intended to stop at San Remo, but she had not known where she had stopped when she asked what place it was. She was consciously an invalid of some sort, for she spoke of getting well under sunsets like that which had now waned, but what sort of invalid was she?

II   Lanfear's question persisted through the night, and it helped, with the coughing in the next room, to make a bad night for him. None of the hotels in San Remo receive consumptive patients, but none are without somewhere a bronchial cough. If it is in the room next yours it keeps you awake, but it is not pulmonary; you may comfort yourself in your vigils with that fact. Lanfear, however, fancied he had got a poor dinner, and in the morning he did not like his coffee. He thought he had let a foolish scruple keep him from the Grand Hotel Sardegna, and he walked down towards it along the palm-flanked promenade, in the gay morning light, with the tideless sea on the other hand lapping the rough beach beyond the lines of the railroad which borders it. On his way he met files of

the beautiful Ligurian women, moving straight under
the burdens balanced on their heads, or bestriding the
donkeys laden with wine-casks in the roadway, or
following beside the carts which the donkeys drew.
Ladies of all nations, in the summer fashions of
London, Berlin, St. Petersburg, Paris, and New York
thronged the path. The sky was of a blue so deep, so
liquid that it seemed to him he could scoop it in his
hand and pour it out again like water. Seaward, he
glanced at the fishing-boats lying motionless in the
offing, and the coastwise steamer that runs between
Nice and Genoa trailing a thin plume of smoke
between him and their white sails. With the more
definite purpose of making sure of the Grand Hotel
Sardegna, he scanned the different villa slopes that
showed their level lines of white and yellow and dull
pink through the gray tropical greenery on the
different levels of the hills. He was duly rewarded by
the sight of the bold legend topping its cornice, and
when he let his eye descend the garden to a little
pavilion on the wall overlooking the road, he saw his
acquaintances of the evening before making a belated
breakfast. The father recognized Lanfear first and
spoke to his daughter, who looked up from her coffee
and down towards him where he wavered, lifting his
hat, and bowed smiling to him. He had no reason to
cross the roadway towards the white stairway which
climbed from it to the hotel grounds, but he did so.
The father leaned out over the wall, and called down
to him: "Won't you come up and join us, doctor?"

"Why, yes!" Lanfear consented, and in another moment he was shaking hands with the girl, to whom, he noticed, her father named him again. He had in his glad sense of her white morning dress and her hat of green-leafed lace, a feeling that she was somehow meeting him as a friend of indefinite date in an intimacy unconditioned by any past or future time. Her pleasure in his being there was as frank as her father's, and there was a pretty trust of him in every word and tone which forbade misinterpretation.

"I was just talking about you, doctor," the father began, "and saying what a pity you hadn't come to our hotel. It's a capital place."

"*I've* been thinking it was a pity I went to mine," Lanfear returned, "though I'm in San Remo for such a short time it's scarcely worth while to change."

"Well, perhaps if you came here, you might stay longer. I guess we're booked for the winter, Nannie?" He referred the question to his daughter, who asked Lanfear if he would not have some coffee.

"I was going to say I had had my coffee, but I'm not sure it *was* coffee," Lanfear began, and he consented, with some demur, banal enough, about the trouble.

"Well, that's right, then, and no trouble at all," Mr. Gerald broke in upon him. "Here comes a fellow looking for a chance to bring you some," and he called to a waiter wandering distractedly about with a "Heigh!" that might have been offensive from a less obviously inoffensive man. "Can you get our friend here a cup and saucer, and some of this good coffee?" he asked, as the waiter approached.

"Yes, certainly, sir," the man answered in careful English. "Is it not, perhaps, Mr. and Misses Gerald?" he smilingly insinuated, offering some cards.

"Miss Gerald," the father corrected him as he took the cards. "Why, hello, Nannie! Here are the Bells! Where are they?" he demanded of the waiter. "Bring them here, and a lot more cups and saucers. Or, hold on! I'd better go myself, Nannie, hadn't I? Of course! You get the crockery, waiter. Where did you say they were?" He bustled up from his chair, without waiting for a distinct reply, and apologized to Lanfear in hurrying away. "You'll excuse me, doctor! I'll be back in half a minute. Friends of ours that came over on the same boat. I must see them, of course, but I don't believe they'll stay. Nannie, don't let Dr. Lanfear get away. I want to have some talk with him. You tell him he'd better come to the Sardegna, here."

Lanfear and Miss Gerald sat a moment in the silence which is apt to follow with young people when they are unexpectedly left to themselves. She kept absently pushing the cards her father had given her up and down on the table between her thumb and forefinger, and Lanfear noted the translucence of her long, thin hand in the sunshine striking across the painted iron surface of the garden movable. The translucence had a pathos for his intelligence which the pensive tilt of her head enhanced. She stopped toying with the cards, and looked at the addresses on them.

"What strange things names are!" she said, as if musing on the fact, with a sigh which he thought disproportioned to the depth of her remark.

"They seem rather irrelevant at times," he admitted, with a smile. "They're mere tags, labels, which can be attached to one as well as another; they seem to belong equally to anybody."

"That is what I always say to myself," she agreed, with more interest than he found explicable.

"But finally," he returned, "they're all that's left us, if they're left themselves. They are the only signs to the few who knew us that we ever existed. They stand for our characters, our personality, our mind, our soul."

She said, "That is very true," and then she suddenly gave him the cards. "Do you know these people?"

"I? I thought they were friends of yours," he replied, astonished.

"That is what papa thinks," Miss Gerald said, and while she sat dreamily absent, a rustle of skirts and a flutter of voices pierced from the surrounding shrubbery, and then a lively matron, of as youthful a temperament as the lively girls she brought in her train, burst upon them, and Miss Gerald was passed from one embrace to another until all four had kissed her. She returned their greeting, and shared, in her quieter way, their raptures at their encounter.

"Such a hunt as we've had for you!" the matron

shouted. "We've been up-stairs and down-stairs and in my lady's chamber, all over the hotel. Where's your father? Ah, they did get our cards to you!" and by that token Lanfear knew that these ladies were the Bells. He had stood up in a sort of expectancy, but Miss Gerald did not introduce him, and a shadow of embarrassment passed over the party which she seemed to feel least, though he fancied a sort of entreaty in the glance that she let pass over him.

"I suppose he's gone to look for *us*!" Mrs. Bell saved the situation with a protecting laugh. Miss Gerald colored intelligently, and Lanfear could not let Mrs. Bell's implication pass.

"If it is Mrs. Bell," he said, "I can answer that he has. I met you at Magnolia some years ago, Mrs. Bell. Dr. Lanfear."

"Oh, I beg your pardon, Dr. Lanfear," Miss Gerald said. "I couldn't think—"

"Of my tag, my label?" he laughed back. "It isn't very distinctly lettered."

Mrs. Bell was not much minding them jointly. She was singling Lanfear out for the expression of her pleasure in seeing him again, and recalling the incidents of her summer at Magnolia before, it seemed, any of her girls were out. She presented them collectively, and the eldest of them charmingly reminded Lanfear that he had once had the magnanimity to dance with her when she sat, in a little girl's forlorn despair of being danced with, at one of those desolate hops of the good old Osprey House.

"Yes; and now," her mother followed, "we can't wait a moment longer, if we're to get our train for Monte Carlo, girls. We're not going to play, doctor," she made time to explain, "but we are going to look on. Will you tell your father, dear," she said, taking the girl's hands caressingly in hers, and drawing her to her motherly bosom, "that we found you, and did our best to find him? We can't wait now—our carriage is champing the bit at the foot of the stairs—but we're coming back in a week, and then we'll do our best to look you up again." She included Lanfear in her good-bye, and all her girls said good-bye in the same way, and with a whisking of skirts and twitter of voices they vanished through the shrubbery, and faded into the general silence and general sound like a bevy of birds which had swept near and passed by.

Miss Gerald sank quietly into her place, and sat as if nothing had happened, except that she looked a little paler to Lanfear, who remained on foot trying to piece together their interrupted tête-à-tête, but not succeeding, when her father reappeared, red and breathless, and wiping his forehead. "Have they been here, Nannie?" he asked. "I've been following them all over the place, and the *portier* told me just now that he had seen a party of ladies coming down this way."

He got it all out, not so clearly as those women had got everything in, Lanfear reflected, but unmistakably enough as to the fact, and he looked at his daughter as he repeated: "Haven't the Bells been here?"

She shook her head, and said, with her delicate

quiet: "Nobody has been here, except—" She glanced at Lanfear, who smiled, but saw no opening for himself in the strange situation. Then she said: "I think I will go and lie down a while, now, papa. I'm rather tired. Good-bye," she said, giving Lanfear her hand; it felt limp and cold; and then she turned to her father again. "Don't you come, papa! I can get back perfectly well by myself. Stay with—"

"I will go with you," her father said, "and if Dr. Lanfear doesn't mind coming—"

"Certainly I will come," Lanfear said, and he passed to the girl's right; she had taken her father's arm; but he wished to offer more support if it were needed. When they had climbed to the open flowery space before the hotel, she seemed aware of the groups of people about. She took her hand from her father's arm, as if unwilling to attract their notice by seeming to need its help, and swept up the gravelled path between him and Lanfear, with her flowing walk.

Her father fell back, as they entered the hotel door, and murmured to Lanfear: "Will you wait till I come down?"… "I wanted to tell you about my daughter," he explained, when he came back after the quarter of an hour which Lanfear had found rather intense. "It's useless to pretend you wouldn't have noticed—Had nobody been with you after I left you, down there?" He twisted his head in the direction of the pavilion, where they had been breakfasting.

"Yes; Mrs. Bell and her daughters," Lanfear answered, simply.

"Of course! Why do you suppose my daughter denied it?" Mr. Gerald asked.

"I suppose she—had her reasons," Lanfear answered, lamely enough.

"No *reason*, I'm afraid," Mr. Gerald said, and he broke out hopelessly: "She has her mind sound enough, but not—not her memory. She had forgotten that they were there! Are you going to stay in San Remo?" he asked, with an effect of interrupting himself, as if in the wish to put off something, or to make the ground sure before he went on.

"Why," Lanfear said, "I hadn't thought of it. I stopped—I was going to Nice—to test the air for a friend who wishes to bring his invalid wife here, if I approve—but I have just been asking myself why I should go to Nice when I could stay at San Remo. The place takes my fancy. I'm something of an invalid myself—at least I'm on my vacation—and I find a charm in it, if nothing better. Perhaps a charm is enough. It used to be, in primitive medicine."

He was talking to what he felt was not an undivided attention in Mr. Gerald, who said, "I'm glad of it," and then added: "I should like to consult you professionally. I know your reputation in New York—though I'm not a New-Yorker myself—and I don't know any of the doctors here. I suppose I've done rather a wild thing in coming off the way I have, with my daughter; but I felt that I must do something, and I hoped—I felt as if it were getting away from our trouble. It's most fortunate my meeting you, if you can look into the case, and help me out with a nurse, if she's needed, and all that!" To a certain hesitation in Lanfear's face, he added: "Of course, I'm asking your professional help. My name is Abner Gerald—Abner L. Gerald—perhaps you know my standing, and that I'm able to—"

"Oh, it isn't a question of that! I shall be glad to do anything I can," Lanfear said, with a little pang which he tried to keep silent in orienting himself anew towards the girl, whose loveliness he had felt before he had felt her piteousness.

"But before you go further I ought to say that you must have been thinking of my uncle, the first Matthew Lanfear, when you spoke of my reputation; I haven't got any yet; I've only got my uncle's name."

"Oh!" Mr. Gerald said, disappointedly, but after a blank moment he apparently took courage. "You're in the same line, though?"

"If you mean the psychopathic line, without being exactly an alienist, well, yes," Lanfear admitted.

"That's exactly what I mean," the elder said, with renewed hopefulness. "I'm quite willing to risk myself with a man of the same name as Dr. Lanfear. I should like," he said, hurrying on, as if to override any further reluctance of Lanfear's, "to tell you her story, and then—"

"By all means," Lanfear consented, and he put on an air of professional deference, while the older man began with a face set for the task.

"It's a long story, or it's a short story, as you choose to make it. We'll make it long, if necessary, later, but now I'll make it short. Five months ago my wife was killed before my daughter's eyes—"

He stopped; Lanfear breathed a gentle "Oh!" and Gerald blurted out:

"Accident—grade crossing—Don't!" he winced at the kindness in Lanfear's eyes, and panted on. "That's over! What happened to *her*—to my daughter—was that she fainted from the shock. When she woke—it was more like a sleep than a swoon—she didn't remember what had happened." Lanfear nodded, with a gravely interested face. "She didn't remember anything that had ever happened before. She knew me, because I was there with her; but she didn't know that she ever had a mother, because she was not there with her. You see?"

"I can imagine," Lanfear assented.

"The whole of her life before the—accident was wiped out as to the facts, as completely as if it had never been; and now every day, every hour, every minute, as it passes, goes with that past. But her faculties—"

"Yes?" Lanfear prompted in the pause which Mr. Gerald made.

"Her intellect—the working powers of her mind, apart from anything like remembering, are as perfect as if she were in full possession of her memory. I believe," the father said, with a pride that had its pathos, "no one can talk with her and not feel that she has a beautiful mind, that she can think better than most girls of her age. She reads, or she lets me read to her, and until it has time to fade, she appreciates it all more fully than I do. At Genoa, where I took her to the palaces for the pictures, I saw that she had kept her feeling for art. When she plays—you will hear her play—it is like composing the music for herself; she does not seem to remember the pieces, she seems to improvise them. You understand?"

Lanfear said that he understood, for he could not disappoint the expectation of the father's boastful love: all that was left him of the ambitions he must once have had for his child.

The poor, little, stout, unpicturesque elderly man got up and began to walk to and fro in the room which he had turned into with Lanfear, and to say, more to himself than to Lanfear, as if balancing one thing against another: "The merciful thing is that she has been saved from the horror and the sorrow. She knows no more of either than she knows of her mother's love for her. They were very much alike in looks and mind, and they were always together more like persons of the same age—sisters, or girl friends; but she has lost all knowledge of that, as of other things. And then there is the question whether she won't some time, sooner or later, come into both the horror and the sorrow." He stopped and looked at Lanfear. "She has these sudden fits of drowsiness, when she *must* sleep; and I never see her wake from them without being afraid that she has wakened to everything—that she has got back into her full self, and taken up the terrible burden that my old shoulders are used to. What do you think?"

Lanfear felt the appeal so keenly that in the effort to answer faithfully he was aware of being harsher than he meant. "That is a chance we can't forecast. But it is a chance. The fact that the drowsiness recurs periodically—"

"It doesn't," the father pleaded. "We don't know when it will come on."

"It scarcely matters. The periodicity wouldn't affect the possible result which you dread. I don't say that it is probable. But it's one of the possibilities. It has," Lanfear added, "its logic."

"Ah, its logic!"

"Its logic, yes. My business, of course, would be to restore her to health at any risk. So far as her mind is affected—"

"Her mind is not affected!" the father retorted.

"I beg your pardon—her memory—it might be restored with her physical health. You understand that? It is a chance; it might or it might not happen."

The father was apparently facing a risk which he had not squarely faced before. "I suppose so," he faltered. After a moment he added, with more courage: "You must do the best you can, at any risk."

Lanfear rose, too. He said, with returning kindness in his tones, if not his words: "I should like to study the case, Mr. Gerald. It's very interesting, and—and—if you'll forgive me—very touching."

"Thank you."

"If you decide to stay in San Remo, I will—Do you suppose I could get a room in this hotel? I don't like mine."

"Why, I haven't any doubt you can. Shall we ask?"

III   It was from the Hotel Sardegna that Lanfear satisfied his conscience by pushing his search for climate on behalf of his friend's neurasthenic wife. He decided that Ospedaletti, with a milder air and more sheltered seat in its valley of palms, would be better for her than San Remo. He wrote his friend to that effect, and then there was no preoccupation to hinder him in his devotion to the case of Miss Gerald. He put the case first in the order of interest rather purposely, and even with a sense of effort, though he could not deny to himself that a like case related to a different personality might have been less absorbing. But he tried to keep his scientific duty to it pure of that certain painful pleasure which, as a young man not much over thirty, he must feel in the strange affliction of a young and beautiful girl.

Though there was no present question of medicine, he could be installed near her, as the friend that her father insisted upon making him, without contravention of the social formalities. His care of her hardly differed from that of her father, except that it involved a closer and more premeditated study. They did not try to keep her from the sort of association which, in a large hotel of the type of the Sardegna, entails no sort of obligation to intimacy. They sat together at the long table, midway of the dining-room, which maintained the tradition of the old table-d'hôte against the small tables ranged along the walls. Gerald had an amiable old man's liking for talk, and Lanfear saw that he willingly escaped, among their changing companions, from the pressure of his anxieties. He left his daughter very much to Lanfear, during these excursions, but Lanfear was far from meaning to keep her to himself. He thought it better that she should follow her father in his forays among their neighbors, and he encouraged her to continue such talk with them as she might be brought into. He tried to guard her future encounters with them, so that she should not show more than a young girl's usual diffidence at a second meeting; and in the frequent substitution of one presence for another across the table, she was fairly safe.

A natural light-heartedness, of which he had glimpses from the first, returned to her. One night, at the dance given by some of the guests to some others, she went through the gayety in joyous triumph. She danced mostly with Lanfear, but she had other partners, and she won a pleasing popularity by the American quality of her waltzing. Lanfear had already noted that her forgetfulness was not always so constant or so inclusive as her father had taught him to expect; Mr. Gerald's statement had been the large, general fact from which there was sometimes a shrinking in the particulars. While the warmth of an agreeable experience lasted, her mind kept record of it, slight or full; if the experience were unpleasant the memory was more apt to fade at once. After that dance she repeated to her father the little compliments paid her, and told him, laughing, they were to reward him for sitting up so late as her chaperon. Emotions persisted in her consciousness as the tremor lasts in a smitten cord, but events left little trace. She retained a sense of personalities; she was lastingly sensible of temperaments; but names were nothing to her. She could not tell her father who had said the nice things to her, and their joint study of her dancing-card did not help them out.

Her relation to Lanfear, though it might be a subject of international scrutiny, was hardly a subject of censure. He was known as Dr. Lanfear, but he was not at first known as her physician; he was conjectured her cousin or something like that; he might even be her betrothed in the peculiar American arrangement of such affairs. Personally people saw in him a serious-looking young man, better dressed and better mannered than they thought most Americans,

and unquestionably handsomer, with his Spanish skin
and eyes, and his brown beard of the Vandyke cut
which was then already beginning to be rather
belated.

Other Americans in the hotel were few and
transitory; and if the English had any mind about Miss
Gerald different from their mind about other girls, it
would be perhaps to the effect that she was quite
mad; by this they would mean that she was a little
odd; but for the rest they had apparently no mind
about her. With the help of one of the English ladies
her father had replaced the homesick Irish maid
whom he had sent back to New York from Genoa,
with an Italian, and in the shelter of her gay affection
and ignorant sympathy Miss Gerald had a security
supplemented by the easy social environment. If she
did not look very well, she did not differ from most
other American women in that; and if she seemed to
confide herself more severely to the safe-keeping of
her physician, that was the way of all women patients.

Whether the Bells found the spectacle of
depravity at Monte Carlo more attractive than the
smiling face of nature at San Remo or not, they did
not return, but sent for their baggage from their hotel,
and were not seen again by the Geralds. Lanfear's
friend with the invalid wife wrote from Ospedaletti,
with apologies which inculpated him for the
disappointment, that she had found the air impossible
in a single day, and they were off for Cannes. Lanfear
and the Geralds, therefore, continued together in the

hotel without fear or obligation to others, and in an immunity in which their right to breakfast exclusively in that pavilion on the garden wall was almost explicitly conceded. No one, after a few mornings of tacit possession, would have disputed their claim, and there, day after day, in the mild monotony of the December sunshine, they sat and drank their coffee, and talked of the sights which the peasants in the street, and the tourists in the promenade beyond it, afforded. The rows of stumpy palms which separated the road from the walk were not so high but that they had the whole lift of the sea to the horizon where it lost itself in a sky that curved blue as turquoise to the zenith overhead. The sun rose from its morning bath on the left, and sank to its evening bath on the right, and in making its climb of the spacious arc between, shed a heat as great as that of summer, but not the heat of summer, on the pretty world of villas and hotels, towered over by the olive-gray slopes of the pine-clad heights behind and above them. From these tops a fine, keen cold fell with the waning afternoon, which sharpened through the sunset till the dusk; but in the morning the change was from the chill to the glow, and they could sit in their pavilion, under the willowy droop of the eucalyptus-trees which have brought the Southern Pacific to the Riviera, with increasing comfort.

In the restlessness of an elderly man, Gerald sometimes left the young people to their intolerable delays over their coffee, and walked off into the little stone and stucco city below, or went and sat with his cigar on one of the benches under the palm-lined promenade, which the pale northern consumptives shared with the swarthy peasant girls resting from their burdens, and the wrinkled grandmothers of their race passively or actively begging from the strangers.

While she kept her father in sight it seemed that Miss Gerald could maintain her hold of his identity, and one morning she said, with the tender fondness for him which touched Lanfear: "When he sits there among those sick people and poor people, then he knows they are in the world."

She turned with a question graver in her look than usual, and he said: "Yes, we might help them oftener if we could remember that their misery was going on all the time, like some great natural process, day or dark, heat or cold, which seems to stop when we stop thinking of it. Nothing, for us, at least, exists unless it is recalled to us."

"Yes," she said, in her turn, "I have noticed that. But don't you sometimes—sometimes"—she knit her forehead, as if to keep her thought from escaping— "have a feeling as if what you were doing, or saying, or seeing, had all happened before, just as it is now?"

"Oh yes; that occurs to every one."

"But don't you—don't you have hints of things, of ideas, as if you had known them, in some previous existence—"

She stopped, and Lanfear recognized, with a kind of impatience, the experience which young people make much of when they have it, and sometimes pretend to when they have merely heard of it. But there could be no pose or pretence in her. He smilingly suggested:

"'For something is, or something seems,
  Like glimpses of forgotten dreams.'

These weird impressions are no more than that, probably."

"Ah, I don't believe it," the girl said. "They are too real for that. They come too often, and they make me feel as if they would come more fully, some time. If there was a life before this—do you believe there was?—they may be things that happened there. Or they may be things that will happen in a life after this. You believe in *that*, don't you?"

"In a life after this, or their happening in it?"

"Well, both."

Lanfear evaded her, partly. "They could be premonitions, prophecies, of a future life, as easily as fragmentary records of a past life. I suppose we do not begin to be immortal merely after death."

"No." She lingered out the word in dreamy absence, as if what they had been saying had already passed from her thought.

"But, Miss Gerald," Lanfear ventured, "have these impressions of yours grown more definite—fuller, as you say—of late?"

"My impressions?" She frowned at him, as if the

look of interest, more intense than usual in his eyes, annoyed her. "I don't know what you mean."

Lanfear felt bound to follow up her lead, whether she wished it or not. "A good third of our lives here is passed in sleep. I'm not always sure that we are right in treating the mental—for certainly they are mental—experiences of that time as altogether trivial, or insignificant."

She seemed to understand now, and she protested: "But I don't mean dreams. I mean things that really happened, or that really will happen."

"Like something you can give me an instance of? Are they painful things, or pleasant, mostly?"

She hesitated. "They are things that you know happen to other people, but you can't believe would ever happen to you."

"Do they come when you are just drowsing, or just waking from a drowse?"

"They are not dreams," she said, almost with vexation.

"Yes, yes, I understand," he hesitated to retrieve himself. "But *I* have had floating illusions, just before I fell asleep, or when I was sensible of not being quite awake, which seemed to differ from dreams. They were not so dramatic, but they were more pictorial; they were more visual than the things in dreams."

"Yes," she assented. "They are something like that. But I should not call them illusions."

"No. And they represent scenes, events?"

"You said yourself they were not dramatic."

"I meant, represent pictorially."

"No; they are like the landscape that flies back from your train or towards it. I can't explain it," she ended, rising with what he felt a displeasure in his pursuit.

IV   He reported what had passed to her father when Mr. Gerald came back from his stroll into the town, with his hands full of English papers; Gerald had even found a New York paper at the news-stand; and he listened with an apparent postponement of interest.

"I think," Lanfear said, "that she has some shadowy recollection, or rather that the facts come to her in a jarred, confused way—the elements of pictures, not pictures. But I am afraid that my inquiry has offended her."

"I guess not," Gerald said, dryly, as if annoyed. "What makes you think so?"

"Merely her manner. And I don't know that anything is to be gained by such an inquiry."

"Perhaps not," Gerald allowed, with an inattention which vexed Lanfear in his turn.

The elderly man looked up, from where he sat provisionally in the hotel veranda, into Lanfear's face; Lanfear had remained standing. "*I* don't believe she's offended. Or she won't be long. One thing, she'll forget it."

He was right enough, apparently. Miss Gerald came out of the hotel door towards them, smiling equally for both, with the indefinable difference between cognition and recognition habitual in her look. She was dressed for a walk, and she seemed to expect them to go with her. She beamed gently upon Lanfear; there was no trace of umbrage in her sunny gayety. Her face had, as always, its lurking pathos, but in its appeal to Lanfear now there were only trust and the wish of pleasing him.

They started side by side for their walk, while her father drove beside them in one of the little public carriages, mounting to the Berigo Road, through a street of the older San Remo, and issuing on a bare little piazza looking towards the walls and roofs of the mediaeval city, clustered together like cliff-dwellings, and down on the gardens that fell from the villas and the hotels. A parapet kept the path on the roadside nearest the declivities, and from point to point benches were put for the convenient enjoyment of the prospect. Mr. Gerald preferred to take his pleasure from the greater elevation of the seat in his victoria; his daughter and Lanfear leaned on the wall, and looked up to the sky and out to the sea, both of the same blue.

The palms and eucalyptus-trees darkened about the villas; the bits of vineyard, in their lingering crimson or lingering gold, and the orchards of peaches and persimmons enriched with the varying reds of their ripening leaves and fruits the enchanting color scheme. The rose and geranium hedges were in bloom; the feathery green of the pepper-trees was warmed by the red-purple of their grape-like clusters of blossoms; the perfume of lemon flowers wandered vaguely upwards from some point which they could not fix.

Nothing of all the beauty seemed lost upon the girl, so bereft that she could enjoy no part of it from association. Lanfear observed that she was not fatigued by any such effort as he was always helplessly making to match what he saw with something he had seen before. Now, when this effort betrayed itself, she said, smiling: "How strange it is that you see things for what they are like, and not for what they are!"

"Yes, it's a defect, I'm afraid, sometimes. Perhaps—"

"Perhaps what?" she prompted him in the pause he made.

"Nothing. I was wondering whether in some other possible life our consciousness would not be more independent of what we have been than it seems to be here." She looked askingly at him. "I mean whether there shall not be something absolute in our existence, whether it shall not realize itself more in each experience of the moment, and not be always seeking to verify itself from the past."

"Isn't that what you think is the way with me already?" She turned upon him smiling, and he perceived that in her New York version of a Parisian costume, with her lace hat of summer make and texture and the vivid parasol she twirled upon her shoulder, she was not only a very pretty girl, but a fashionable one. There was something touching in the fact, and a little bewildering. To the pretty girl, the fashionable girl, he could have answered with a joke, but the stricken intelligence had a claim to his seriousness. Now, especially, he noted what had from time to time urged itself upon his perception. If the broken ties which once bound her to the past were beginning to knit again, her recovery otherwise was not apparent. As she stood there her beauty had signally the distinction of fragility, the delicacy of shattered nerves in which there was yet no visible return to strength. A feeling, which had intimated itself before, a sense as of being in the presence of a disembodied spirit, possessed him, and brought, in its contradiction of an accepted theory, a suggestion that was destined to become conviction. He had always said to himself that there could be no persistence of personality, of character, of identity, of consciousness, except through memory; yet here, to the last implication of temperament, they all persisted. The soul that was passing in its integrity through time without the helps, the crutches, of remembrance by which his own personality supported itself, why should not it pass so through eternity without that loss of identity which was equivalent to annihilation?

Her waiting eyes recalled him from his inquiry, and with an effort he answered, "Yes, I think you do have your being here and now, Miss Gerald, to an unusual degree."

"And you don't think that is wrong?"

"Wrong? Why? How?"

"Oh, I don't know." She looked round, and her eye fell upon her father waiting for them in his carriage beside the walk. The sight supplied her with the notion which Lanfear perceived would not have occurred otherwise. "Then why doesn't papa want me to remember things?"

"I don't know," Lanfear temporized. "Doesn't he?"

"I can't always tell. Should—should *you* wish me to remember more than I do?"

"I?"

She looked at him with entreaty. "Do you think it would make my father happier if I did?"

"That I can't say," Lanfear answered. "People are often the sadder for what they remember. If I were your father—Excuse me! I don't mean anything so absurd. But in his place—"

He stopped, and she said, as if she were satisfied with his broken reply: "It is very curious. When I look at him—when I am with him—I know him; but when he is away, I don't remember him." She seemed rather interested in the fact than distressed by it; she even smiled.

"And me," he ventured, "is it the same with regard to me?"

She did not say; she asked, smiling: "Do you remember me when I am away?"

"Yes!" he answered. "As perfectly as if you were with me. I can see you, hear you, feel the touch of your hand, your dress—Good heavens!" he added to himself under his breath. "What am I saying to this poor child!"

In the instinct of escaping from himself he started forward, and she moved with him. Mr. Gerald's watchful driver followed them with the carriage.

"That is very strange," she said, lightly. "Is it so with you about everyone?"

"No," he replied, briefly, almost harshly. He asked, abruptly: "Miss Gerald, are there any times when you know people in their absence?"

"Just after I wake from a nap—yes. But it doesn't last. That is, it seems to me it doesn't. I'm not sure."

As they followed the winding of the pleasant way, with the villas on the slopes above and on the slopes below, she began to talk of them, and to come into that knowledge of each which formed her remembrance of them from former knowledge of them, but which he knew would fade when she passed them.

The next morning, when she came down unwontedly late to breakfast in their pavilion, she called gayly:

"Dr. Lanfear! It *is* Dr. Lanfear?"

"I should be sorry if it were not, since you seem to expect it, Miss Gerald."

"Oh, I just wanted to be sure. Hasn't my father been here, yet?" It was the first time she had shown herself aware of her father except in his presence, as it was the first time she had named Lanfear to his face.

He suppressed a remote stir of anxiety, and answered: "He went to get his newspapers; he wished you not to wait. I hope you slept well?"

"Splendidly. But I was very tired last night; I don't know why, exactly."

"We had rather a long walk."

"Did we have a walk yesterday?"

"Yes."

"Then it was *so*! I thought I had dreamed it. I was beginning to remember something, and my father asked me what it was, and then I couldn't remember. Do you believe I shall keep on remembering?"

"I don't see why you shouldn't."

"Should you wish me to?" she asked, in evident, however unconscious, recurrence to their talk of the day before.

"Why not?"

She sighed. "I don't know. If it's like some of those dreams or gleams. Is remembering pleasant?"

Lanfear thought for a moment. Then he said, in the honesty he thought best to use with her: "For the most part I should say it was painful. Life is tolerable enough while it passes, but when it is past, what remains seems mostly to hurt and humiliate. I don't know why we should remember so insistently the foolish things and wrong things we do, and not recall the times when we acted, without an effort, wisely and rightly." He thought he had gone too far, and he hedged a little. "I don't mean that we *can't* recall those times. We can and do, to console and encourage ourselves; but they don't recur, without our willing, as the others do."

She had poured herself a cup of coffee, and she played with the spoon in her saucer while she seemed to listen. But she could not have been listening, for when she put down her spoon and leaned back in her chair, she said: "In those dreams the things come from such a very far way back, and they don't belong to a life that is like this. They belong to a life like what you hear the life after this is. We are the same as we are here; but the things are different. We haven't the same rules, the same wishes—I can't explain."

"You mean that we are differently conditioned?"

"Yes. And if you can understand, I feel as if I remembered long back of this, and long forward of this. But one can't remember forward!"

"That wouldn't be remembrance; no, it would be prescience; and your consciousness here, as you were saying yesterday, is through knowing, not remembering."

She stared at him. "Was that yesterday? I thought it was—tomorrow." She rubbed her hand across her forehead as people do when they wish to clear their minds. Then she sighed deeply. "It tires me so. And yet I can't help trying." A light broke over her face at the sound of a step on the gravel walk near by, and she said, laughing, without looking round: "That is papa! I knew it was his step."

V   Such return of memory as she now had was like memory in what we call the lower lives. It increased, fluctuantly, with an ebb in which it almost disappeared, but with a flow that in its advance carried it beyond its last flood-tide mark. After the first triumph in which she could address Lanfear by his name, and could greet her father as her father, there were lapses in which she knew them as before, without naming them. Except mechanically to repeat the names of other people when reminded of them, she did not pass beyond cognition to recognition. Events still left no trace upon her; or if they did she was not sure whether they were things she had dreamed or experienced. But her memory grew stronger in the region where the bird knows its way home to the nest, or the bee to the hive. She had an unerring instinct for places where she had once been, and she found her way to them again without the help from the association which sometimes failed Lanfear. Their walks were always taken with her father's company in his carriage, but they sometimes left him at a point of the Berigo Road, and after a long détour among the vineyards and olive orchards of the heights above, rejoined him at another point they had agreed upon with him. One afternoon, when Lanfear had climbed the rough pave of the footways with her to one of the summits, they stopped to rest on the wall of a terrace, where they sat watching the changing light on the sea, through a break in the trees. The shadows surprised them on their height, and they had to make their way among them over the farm paths and by the dry beds of the torrents to the carriage road far below. They had been that walk only once before, and Lanfear failed of his reckoning, except the downward course which must bring them out on the high-road at last. But Miss Gerald's instinct saved them where his reason failed. She did not remember, but she knew the way, and she led him on as if she were inventing it, or as if it had been indelibly traced upon her mind and she had only to follow the mystical lines within to be sure of her course. She confessed to being very tired, and each step must have increased her fatigue, but each step seemed to clear her perception of the next to be taken.

Suddenly, when Lanfear was blaming himself for

bringing all this upon her, and then for trusting to her guidance, he recognized a certain peasant's house, and in a few moments they had descended the olive-orchard terraces to a broken cistern in the clear twilight beyond the dusk. She suddenly halted him. "There, there! It happened then—now—this instant!"

"What?"

"That feeling of being here before! There is the curb of the old cistern; and the place where the terrace wall is broken; and the path up to the vineyard—Don't you feel it, too?" she demanded, with a joyousness which had no pleasure for him.

"Yes, certainly. We were here last week. We went up the path to the farm-house to get some water."

"Yes, now I am remembering—remembering!" She stood with eagerly parted lips, and glancing quickly round with glowing eyes, whose light faded in the same instant. "No!" she said, mournfully, "it's gone."

A sound of wheels in the road ceased, and her father's voice called: "Don't you want to take my place, and let me walk awhile, Nannie?"

"No. You come to me, papa. Something very strange has happened; something you will be surprised at. Hurry!" She seemed to be joking, as he was, while she beckoned him impatiently towards her.

He had left his carriage, and he came up with a heavy man's quickened pace. "Well, what is the wonderful thing?" he panted out.

She stared blankly at him, without replying, and they silently made their way to Mr. Gerald's carriage.

"I lost the way, and Miss Gerald found it," Lanfear explained, as he helped her to the place beside her father.

She said nothing, and almost with sinking into the seat, she sank into that deep slumber which from time to time overtook her.

"I didn't know we had gone so far—or rather that we had waited so long before we started down the hills," Lanfear apologized in an involuntary whisper.

"Oh, it's all right," her father said, trying to adjust the girl's fallen head to his shoulder. "Get in and help me—"

Lanfear obeyed, and lent a physician's skilled aid, which left the cumbrous efforts of her father to the blame he freely bestowed on them. "You'll have to come here on the other side," he said. "There's room enough for all three. Or, hold on! Let me take your place." He took the place in front, and left her to Lanfear's care, with the trust which was the physician's right, and with a sense of the girl's dependence in which she was still a child to him.

They did not speak till well on the way home. Then the father leaned forward and whispered huskily: "Do you think she's as strong as she was?"

Lanfear waited, as if thinking the facts over. He murmured back: "No. She's better. She's not so strong."

"Yes," the father murmured. "I understand."

What Gerald understood by Lanfear's words might not have been their meaning, but what Lanfear meant was that there was now an interfusion of the past and present in her daily experience. She still did not remember, but she had moments in which she hovered upon such knowledge of what had happened as she had of actual events. When she was stronger she seemed farther from this knowledge; when she was weaker she was nearer it. So it seemed to him in that region where he could be sure of his own duty when he looked upon it singly as concern for her health. No inquiry for the psychological possibilities must be suffered to divide his effort for her physical recovery, though there might come with this a cessation of the timeless dream-state in which she had her being, and she might sharply realize the past, as the anaesthete realizes his return to agony from insensibility. The quality of her mind was as different from the thing called culture as her manner from convention. A simplicity beyond the simplicity of childhood was one with a poetic color in her absolute ideas. But this must cease with her restoration to the strength in which she could alone come into full and clear self-consciousness. So far as Lanfear could give reality to his occupation with her disability, he was ministering to a mind diseased; not to "rase out its written trouble," but if possible to restore the obliterated record, and enable her to spell its tragic characters. If he could, he would have shrunk from this office; but all the more because he specially had to do with the mystical side of medicine, he always tried to keep his relation to her free from personal feeling, and his aim single and matter-of-fact.

It was hard to do this; and there was a glamour in the very topographical and meteorological environment. The autumn was a long delight in which the constant sea, the constant sky, knew almost as little variance as the unchanging Alps. The days passed in a procession of sunny splendor, neither hot nor cold, nor of the temper of any determinate season, unless it were an abiding spring-time. The flowers bloomed, and the grass kept green in a reverie of May. But one afternoon of January, while Lanfear was going about in a thin coat and panama hat, a soft, fresh wind began to blow from the east. It increased till sunset, and then fell. In the morning he looked out on a world in which the spring had stiffened overnight into winter. A thick frost painted the leaves and flowers; icicles hung from pipes and vents; the frozen streams flashed back from their arrested flow the sun as it shone from the cold heaven, and blighted and blackened the hedges of geranium and rose, the borders of heliotrope, the fields of pinks. The leaves of the bananas hung limp about their stems; the palms rattled like skeletons in the wind when it began to blow again over the shrunken landscape.

VI   The caprice of a climate which vaunted itself
     perpetual summer was a godsend to all the strangers
     strong enough to bear it without suffering. For the
     sick an indoor life of huddling about the ineffectual
     fires of the south began, and lasted for the fortnight
     that elapsed before the Riviera got back its advertised
     temperature. Miss Gerald had drooped in the milder
     weather; but the cold braced and lifted her, and with
     its help she now pushed her walks farther, and was
     eager every day for some excursion to the little towns
     that whitened along the shores, or the villages that
     glimmered from the olive-orchards of the hills. Once
     she said to Lanfear, when they were climbing through
     the brisk, clear air: "It seems to me as if I had been
     here before. Have I?"

"No. This is the first time."

She said no more, but seemed disappointed in his answer, and he suggested: "Perhaps it is the cold that reminds you of our winters at home, and makes you feel that the scene is familiar."

"Yes, that is it!" she returned, joyously. "Was there snow, there, like that on the mountains yonder?"

"A good deal more, I fancy. That will be gone in a few days, and at home, you know, our snow lasts for weeks."

"Then that is what I was thinking of," she said, and she ran strongly and lightly forward. "Come!"

When the harsh weather passed and the mild climate returned there was no lapse of her strength. A bloom, palely pink as the flowers that began to flush the almond-trees, came upon her delicate beauty, a light like that of the lengthening days dawned in her eyes. She had an instinct for the earliest violets among the grass under the olives; she was first to hear the blackcaps singing in the garden-tops; and nothing that was novel in her experience seemed alien to it. This was the sum of what Lanfear got by the questioning which he needlessly tried to keep indirect. She knew that she was his patient, and in what manner, and she had let him divine that her loss of memory was suffering as well as deprivation. She had not merely the fatigue which we all undergo from the effort to recall things, and which sometimes reaches exhaustion; but there was apparently in the void of her oblivion a perpetual rumor of events, names, sensations, like—Lanfear felt that he inadequately conjectured—the subjective noises which are always in the ears of the deaf. Sometimes, in the distress of it, she turned to him for help, and when he was able to guess what she was striving for, a radiant relief and gratitude transfigured her face. But this could not last, and he learned to note how soon the stress and tension of her effort returned. His compassion for her at such times involved a temptation, or rather a question, which he had to silence by a direct effort of his will. Would it be worse, would it be greater anguish for her to know at once the past that now tormented her consciousness with its broken and meaningless reverberations? Then he realized that it was impossible to help her even through the hazard of telling her what had befallen; that no such effect as was to be desired could be anticipated from the outside.

If he turned to her father for counsel or instruction, or even a participation in his responsibility, he was met by an optimistic patience which exasperated him, if it did not complicate the case. Once, when Lanfear forbearingly tried to share with him his anxiety for the effect of a successful event, he was formed to be outright, and remind him, in so many words, that the girl's restoration might be through anguish which he could not measure.

Gerald faltered aghast; then he said: "It mustn't come to that; you mustn't let it."

"How do you expect me to prevent it?" Lanfear demanded, in his vexation.

Gerald caught his breath. "If she gets well, she will remember?"

"I don't say that. It seems probable. Do you wish her being to remain bereft of one-half its powers?"

"Oh, how do I know what I want?" the poor man groaned. "I only know that I trust you entirely, Doctor Lanfear. Whatever you think best will be best and wisest, no matter what the outcome is."

He got away from Lanfear with these hopeless words, and again Lanfear perceived that the case was left wholly to him. His consolation was the charm of the girl's companionship, the delight of a nature knowing itself from moment to moment as if newly created. For her, as nearly as he could put the fact into words, the actual moment contained the past and the future as well as the present. When he saw in her the persistence of an exquisite personality independent of the means by which he realized his own continuous identity, he sometimes felt as if in the presence of some angel so long freed from earthly allegiance that it had left all record behind, as we leave here the records of our first years. If an echo of the past reached her, it was apt to be trivial and insignificant, like those unimportant experiences of our remotest childhood, which remain to us from a world outlived.

It was not an insipid perfection of character which reported itself in these celestial terms, and Lanfear conjectured that angelic immortality, if such a thing were, could not imply perfection except at the cost of one-half of human character. When the girl wore a dress that she saw pleased him more than another, there was a responsive pleasure in her eyes, which he could have called vanity if he would; and she had at times a wilfulness which he could have accused of being obstinacy. She showed a certain jealousy of any experiences of his apart from her own, not because they included others, but because they excluded her. He was aware of an involuntary vigilance in her, which could not leave his motives any more than his actions unsearched. But in her conditioning she could not repent; she could only offer him at some other time the unconscious reparation of her obedience. The self-criticism which the child has not learned she had forgotten, but in her oblivion the wish to please existed as perfectly as in the ignorance of childhood.

This, so far as he could ever put into words, was the interior of the world where he dwelt apart with her. Its exterior continued very like that of other worlds where two young people have their being. Now and then a more transitory guest at the Grand Hotel Sardegna perhaps fancied it the iridescent orb which takes the color of the morning sky, and is destined, in the course of nature, to the danger of collapse in which planetary space abounds. Some rumor of this could not fail to reach Lanfear, but he ignored it as best he could in always speaking gravely of Miss Gerald as his patient, and authoritatively treating her as such. He convinced some of these witnesses against their senses; for the others, he felt that it mattered little what they thought, since, if it reached her, it could not pierce her isolation for more than the instant in which the impression from absent things remained to her.

A more positive embarrassment, of a kind Lanfear was not prepared for, beset him in an incident which would have been more touching if he had been less singly concerned for the girl. A pretty English boy, with the dawn of a peachy bloom on his young cheeks, and an impulsiveness commoner with English youth than our own, talked with Miss Gerald one evening and the next day sent her an armful of flowers with his card. He followed this attention with a call at her father's apartment, and after Miss Gerald seemed to know him, and they had, as he told Lanfear, a delightful time together, she took up his card from the table where it was lying, and asked him if he could tell her who that gentleman was. The poor fellow's inference was that she was making fun of him, and he came to Lanfear, as an obvious friend of the family, for an explanation. He reported the incident, with indignant tears standing in his eyes: "What did she mean by it? If she took my flowers, she must have known that—that—they—And to pretend to forget my name! Oh, I say, it's too bad! She could have got rid of me without that. Girls have ways enough, you know."

"Yes, yes," Lanfear assented, slowly, to gain time. "I can assure you that Miss Gerald didn't mean anything that could wound you. She isn't very well— she's rather odd—"

"Do you mean that she's out of her mind? She can talk as well as any one—better!"

"No, not that. But she's often in pain—greatly in pain when she can't recall a name, and I've no doubt she was trying to recall yours with the help of your card. She would be the last in the world to be indifferent to your feelings. I imagine she scarcely knew what she was doing at the moment."

"Then, do you think—do you suppose—it would be any good my trying to see her again? If she wouldn't be indifferent to my feelings, do you think there would be any hope—Really, you know, I would give anything to believe that my feelings wouldn't offend her. You understand me?"

"Perhaps I do."

"I've never met a more charming girl and—she isn't engaged, is she? She isn't engaged to you? I don't mean to press the question, but it's a question of life and death with me, you know."

Lanfear thought he saw his way out of the coil. "I can tell you, quite as frankly as you ask, that Miss Gerald isn't engaged to *me*."

"Then it's somebody else—somebody in America! Well, I hope she'll be happy; *I* never shall." He offered his hand to Lanfear. "I'm off."

"Oh, here's the doctor, now," a voice said behind them where they stood by the garden wall, and they turned to confront Gerald with his daughter.

"Why! Are you going?" she said to the Englishman, and she put out her hand to him.

"Yes, Mr. Evers is going." Lanfear came to the rescue.

"Oh, I'm sorry," the girl said, and the youth responded.

"That's very good of you. I—good-bye! I hope you'll be very happy—I—" He turned abruptly away, and ran into the hotel.

"What has he been crying for?" Miss Gerald asked, turning from a long look after him.

Lanfear did not know quite what to say; but he hazarded saying: "He was hurt that you had forgotten him when he came to see you this afternoon."

"Did he come to see me?" she asked; and Lanfear exchanged looks of anxiety, pain, and reassurance with her father. "I am so sorry. Shall I go after him and tell him?"

"No; I explained; he's all right," Lanfear said.

"You want to be careful, Nannie," her father added, "about people's feelings when you meet them, and afterwards seem not to know them."

"But I *do* know them, papa," she remonstrated.

"You want to be careful," her father repeated.

"I will—I will, indeed." Her lips quivered, and the tears came, which Lanfear had to keep from flowing by what quick turn he could give to something else.

An obscure sense of the painful incident must have lingered with her after its memory had perished. One afternoon when Lanfear and her father went with her to the military concert in the sycamore-planted piazza near the Vacherie Suisse, where they often came for a cup of tea, she startled them by bowing gayly to a young lieutenant of engineers standing there with some other officers, and making the most of the prospect of pretty foreigners which the place afforded. The lieutenant returned the bow with interest, and his eyes did not leave their party as long as they remained. Within the bounds of deference for her, it was evident that his comrades were joking about the honor done him by this charming girl. When the Geralds started homeward Lanfear was aware of a trio of officers following them, not conspicuously, but unmistakably; and after that, he could not start on his walks with Miss Gerald and her father without the sense that the young lieutenant was hovering somewhere in their path, waiting in the hopes of another bow from her. The officer was apparently not discouraged by his failure to win recognition from her, and what was amounting to annoyance for Lanfear reached the point where he felt he must share it with her father. He had nearly as much trouble in imparting it to him as he might have had with Miss Gerald herself. He managed, but when he required her father to put a stop to it he perceived that Gerald was as helpless as she would have been. He first wished to verify the fact from its beginning with her, but this was not easy.

"Nannie," he said, "why did you bow to that officer the other day?"

"What officer, papa? When?"

"You know; there by the band-stand, at the Swiss Dairy."

She stared blankly at him, and it was clear that it was all as if it had not been with her. He insisted, and then she said: "Perhaps I thought I knew him, and was afraid I should hurt his feelings if I didn't recognize him. But I don't remember it at all." The curves of her mouth drooped, and her eyes grieved, so that her father had not the heart to say more. She left them, and when he was alone with Lanfear he said:

"You see how it is!"

"Yes, I saw how it was before. But what do you wish to do?"

"Do you mean that he will keep it up?"

"Decidedly, he'll keep it up. He has every right to from his point of view."

"Oh, well, then, my dear fellow, you must stop it, somehow. You'll know how to do it."

"I?" said Lanfear, indignantly; but his vexation was not so great that he did not feel a certain pleasure in fulfilling this strangest part of his professional duty, when at the beginning of their next excursion he put Miss Gerald into the victoria with her father and fell back to the point at which he had seen the lieutenant waiting to haunt their farther progress. He put himself plumply in front of the officer and demanded in very blunt Italian: "What do you want?"

The lieutenant stared him over with potential offence, in which his delicately pencilled mustache took the shape of a light sneer, and demanded in his turn, in English much better than Lanfear's Italian: "What right have you to ask?"

"The right of Miss Gerald's physician. She is an invalid in my charge."

A change quite indefinable except as the visible transition from coxcomb to gentleman passed over the young lieutenant's comely face. "An invalid?" he faltered.

"Yes," Lanfear began; and then, with a rush of confidence which the change in the officer's face justified, "one very strangely, very tragically afflicted. Since she saw her mother killed in an accident a year ago she remembers nothing. She bowed to you because she saw you looking at her, and supposed you must be an acquaintance. May I assure you that you are altogether mistaken?"

The lieutenant brought his heels together, and bent low. "I beg her pardon with all my heart. I am very, very sorry. I will do anything I can. I would like to stop that. May I bring my mother to call on Miss Gerald?"

He offered his hand, and Lanfear wrung it hard, a lump of gratitude in his throat choking any particular utterance, while a fine shame for his late hostile intention covered him.

When the lieutenant came, with all possible circumstance, bringing the countess, his mother, Mr. Gerald overwhelmed them with hospitality of every form. The Italian lady responded effusively, and more sincerely cooed and murmured her compassionate interest in his daughter. Then all parted the best of friends; but when it was over, Miss Gerald did not know what it had been about. She had not remembered the lieutenant or her father's vexation, or any phase of the incident which was now closed. Nothing remained of it but the lieutenant's right, which he gravely exercised, of saluting them respectfully whenever he met them.

VII   Earlier, Lanfear had never allowed himself to be far out of call from Miss Gerald's father, especially during the daytime slumbers into which she fell, and from which they both always dreaded her awakening. But as the days went on and the event continued the same he allowed himself greater range. Formerly the three went on their walks or drives together, but now he sometimes went alone. In these absences he found relief from the stress of his constant vigilance; he was able to cast off the bond which enslaves the physician to his patient, and which he must ignore at times for mere self-preservation's sake; but there was always a lurking anxiety, which, though he refused to let it define itself to him, shortened the time and space he tried to put between them.

One afternoon in April, when he left her sleeping, he was aware of somewhat recklessly placing himself out of reach in a lonely excursion to a village demolished by the earthquake of 1887, and abandoned himself, in the impressions and incidents of his visit to the ruin, to a luxury of impersonal melancholy which the physician cannot often allow himself. At last, his care found him, and drove him home full of a sharper fear than he had yet felt since the first days. But Mr. Gerald was tranquilly smoking under a palm in the hotel garden, and met him with an easy smile. "She woke once, and said she had had such a pleasant dream. Now she's off again. Do you think we'd better wake her for dinner? I suppose she's getting up her strength in this way. Her sleeping so much is a good symptom, isn't it?"

Lanfear smiled forlornly; neither of them, in view of the possible eventualities, could have said what result they wished the symptoms to favor. But he said: "Decidedly I wouldn't wake her"; and he spent a night of restless sleep penetrated by a nervous expectation which the morning, when it came, rather mockingly defeated.

Miss Gerald appeared promptly at breakfast in their pavilion, with a fresher and gayer look than usual, and to her father's "Well, Nannie, you *have* had a nap, this time," she answered, smiling:

"Have I? It isn't afternoon, is it?"

"No, it's morning. You've napped it all night."

She said: "I can't tell whether I've been asleep or

not, sometimes; but now I know I have been; and I feel so rested. Where are we going to-day?"

She turned to Lanfear while her father answered: "I guess the doctor won't want to go very far, to-day, after his expedition yesterday afternoon."

"Ah," she said, "I *knew* you had been somewhere! Was it very far? Are you too tired?"

"It was rather far, but I'm not tired. I shouldn't advise Possana, though."

"Possana?" she repeated. "What is Possana?"

He told her, and then at a jealous look in her eyes he added an account of his excursion. He heightened, if anything, its difficulties, in making light of them as no difficulties for him, and at the end she said, gently: "Shall we go this morning?"

"Let the doctor rest this morning, Nannie," her father interrupted, whimsically, but with what Lanfear knew to be an inner yielding to her will. "Or if you won't let *him*, let *me*. I don't want to go anywhere this morning."

Lanfear thought that he did not wish her to go at all, and hoped that by the afternoon she would have forgotten Possana. She sighed, but in her sigh there was no concession. Then, with the chance of a returning drowse to save him from openly thwarting her will, he merely suggested: "There's plenty of time in the afternoon; the days are so long now; and we can get the sunset from the hills."

"Yes, that will be nice," she said, but he perceived that she did not assent willingly; and there was an effect of resolution in the readiness with which she appeared dressed for the expedition after luncheon. She clearly did not know where they were going, but when she turned to Lanfear with her look of entreaty, he had not the heart to join her father in any conspiracy against her. He beckoned the carriage which had become conscious in its eager driver from the moment she showed herself at the hotel door, and they set out.

When they had left the higher level of the hotel and began their clatter through the long street of the town, Lanfear noted that she seemed to feel as much as himself the quaintness of the little city, rising on one hand, with its narrow alleys under successive arches between the high, dark houses, to the hills, and dropping on the other to sea from the commonplace of the principal thoroughfare, with its pink and white and saffron hotels and shops. Beyond the town their course lay under villa walls, covered with vines and topped by pavilions, and opening finally along a stretch of the old Cornice road.

"But this," she said, at a certain point, "is where we were yesterday!"

"This is where the doctor was yesterday," her father said, behind his cigar.

"And wasn't I with you?" she asked Lanfear.

He said, playfully: "To-day you are. I mustn't be selfish and have you every day."

"Ah, you are laughing at me; but I know I was here yesterday."

Her father set his lips in patience, and Lanfear did not insist.

They had halted at this point because, across a wide valley on the shoulder of an approaching height, the ruined village of Possana showed, and lower down and nearer the seat the new town which its people had built when they escaped from the destruction of their world-old home.

World-old it all was, with reference to the human life of it; but the spring-time was immortally young in the landscape. Over the expanses of green and brown fields, and hovering about the gray and white cottages, was a mist of peach and cherry blossoms. Above these the hoar olives thickened, and the vines climbed from terrace to terrace. The valley narrowed inland, and ceased in the embrace of the hills drawing mysteriously together in the distances.

"I think we've got the best part of it here, Miss Gerald," Lanfear broke the common silence by saying. "You couldn't see much more of Possana after you got there."

"Besides," her father ventured a pleasantry which jarred on the younger man, "if you were there with the doctor yesterday, you won't want to make the climb again to-day. Give it up, Nannie!"

"Oh no," she said, "I can't give it up."

"Well, then, we must go on, I suppose. Where do we begin our climb?"

Lanfear explained that he had been obliged to leave his carriage at the foot of the hill, and climb to

Possana Nuova by the donkey-paths of the peasants. He had then walked to the ruins of Possana Vecchia, but he suggested that they might find donkeys to carry them on from the new town.

"Well, I hope so," Mr. Gerald grumbled. But at Possana Nuova no saddle-donkeys were to be had, and he announced, at the café where they stopped for the negotiation, that he would wait for the young people to go on to Possana Vecchia, and tell him about it when they got back. In the meantime he would watch the game of ball, which, in the piazza before the café, appeared to have engaged the energies of the male population. Lanfear was still inwardly demurring, when a stalwart peasant girl came in and announced that she had one donkey which they could have with her own services driving it. She had no saddle, but there was a pad on which the young lady could ride.

"Oh, well, take it for Nannie," Mr. Gerald directed; "only don't be gone too long."

They set out with Miss Gerald reclining in the kind of litter which the donkey proved to be equipped with. Lanfear went beside her, the peasant girl came behind, and at times ran forward to instruct them in the points they seemed to be looking at. For the most part the landscape opened beneath them, but in the azure distances it climbed into Alpine heights which the recent snows had now left to the gloom of their pines. On the slopes of the nearer hills little towns clung, here and there; closer yet farmhouses showed themselves among the vines and olives.

It was very simple, as the life in it must always have been; and Lanfear wondered if the elemental charm of the scene made itself felt by his companion as they climbed the angles of the inclines, in a silence broken only by the picking of the donkey's hoofs on the rude mosaic of the pavement, and the panting of the peasant girl at its heels. On the top of the last upward stretch they stopped for the view, and Miss Gerald asked abruptly: "Why were you so sad?"

"When was I sad?" he asked, in turn.

"I don't know. Weren't you sad?"

"When I was here yesterday, you mean?" She smiled on his fortunate guess, and he said: "Oh, I don't know. It might have begun with thinking—

'Of old, unhappy, far-off things,
    And battles long ago.'

"You know the pirates used to come sailing over the peaceful sea yonder from Africa, to harry these coasts, and carry off as many as they could capture into slavery in Tunis and Algiers. It was a long, dumb kind of misery that scarcely made an echo in history, but it haunted my fancy yesterday, and I saw these valleys full of the flight and the pursuit which used to fill them, up to the walls of the villages, perched on the heights where men could have built only for safety. Then, I got to thinking of other things—"

"And thinking of things in the past always makes you sad," she said, in pensive reflection. "If it were not for the wearying of always trying to remember, I don't believe I should want my memory back. And of course to be like other people," she ended with a sigh.

It was on his tongue to say that he would not have her so; but he checked himself, and said, lamely enough: "Perhaps you will be like them, sometime."

She startled him by answering irrelevantly: "You know my mother is dead. She died a long while ago; I suppose I must have been very little."

She spoke as if the fact scarcely concerned her, and Lanfear drew a breath of relief in his surprise. He asked, at another tangent: "What made you think I was sad yesterday?"

"Oh, I knew, somehow. I think that I always know when you are sad; I can't tell you how, but I feel it."

"Then I must cheer up," Lanfear said. "If I could only see you strong and well, Miss Gerald, like this girl—"

They both looked at the peasant, and she laughed in sympathy with their smiling, and beat the donkey a little for pleasure; it did not mind.

"But you will be—you will be! We must hurry on, now, or your father will be getting anxious."

They pushed forward on the road, which was now level and wider than it had been. As they drew near the town, whose ruin began more and more to reveal itself in the roofless walls and windowless casements, they saw a man coming towards them, at whose approach Lanfear instinctively put himself forward. The man did not look at them, but passed, frowning darkly, and muttering and gesticulating.

Miss Gerald turned in her litter and followed him with a long gaze. The peasant girl said gayly in Italian: "He is mad; the earthquake made him mad," and urged the donkey forward.

Lanfear, in the interest of science, habitually forbade himself the luxury of anything like foreboding, but now, with the passing of the madman, he felt distinctively a lift from his spirit. He no longer experienced the vague dread which had followed him towards Possana, and made him glad of any delay that kept them from it.

They entered the crooked, narrow street leading abruptly from the open country without any suburban hesitation into the heart of the ruin, which kept a vivid image of uninterrupted mediaeval life. There, till within the actual generation, people had dwelt, winter and summer, as they had dwelt from the beginning of Christian times, with nothing to intimate a domestic or civic advance. This street must have been the main thoroughfare, for stone-paved lanes, still narrower, wound from it here and there, while it kept a fairly direct course to the little piazza on a height in the midst of the town. Two churches and a simple town house partly enclosed it with their seamed and shattered façades. The dwellings here were more ruinous than on the thoroughfare, and some were tumbled in heaps. But Lanfear pushed open the door of one of the churches, and found himself in an interior which, except that it was roofless, could not have been greatly changed since the people had flocked into it to pray for safety from the earthquake. The high altar stood unshaken; around the frieze a succession of stucco cherubs perched, under the open sky, in celestial security.

He had learned to look for the unexpected in Miss Gerald, and he could not have said that it was with surprise he now found her as capable of the emotions which the place inspired, as himself. He made sure of saying: "The earthquake, you know," and she responded with compassion:

"Oh yes; and perhaps that poor man was here, praying with the rest, when it happened. How strange it must all have seemed to them, here where they lived so safely always! They thought such a dreadful thing could happen to others, but not to them. That is the way!"

It seemed to Lanfear once more that she was on the verge of the knowledge so long kept from her. But she went confidently on like a sleepwalker who saves himself from dangers that would be death to him in waking. She spoke of the earthquake as if she had been reading or hearing of it; but he doubted if, with her broken memory, this could be so. It was rather as if she was exploring his own mind in the way of which he had more than once been sensible, and making use of his memory. From time to time she spoke of remembering, but he knew that this was as the blind speak of seeing.

He was anxious to get away, and at last they came out to where they had left the peasant girl waiting beside her donkey. She was not there, and after trying this way and that in the tangle of alleys, Lanfear decided to take the thoroughfare which they had come up by and trust to the chance of finding her at its foot. But he failed even of his search for the street: he came out again and again at the point he had started from.

"What is the matter?" she asked at the annoyance he could not keep out of his face.

He laughed. "Oh, merely that we're lost. But we will wait here till that girl chooses to come back for us. Only it's getting late, and Mr. Gerald—"

"Why, I know the way down," she said, and started quickly in a direction which, as they kept it, he recognized as the route by which he had emerged from the town the day before. He had once more the sense of his memory being used by her, as if being blind, she had taken his hand for guidance, or as if being herself disabled from writing, she had directed a pen in his grasp to form the words she desired to put down. In some mystical sort the effect was hers, but the means was his.

They found the girl waiting with the donkey by the roadside beyond the last house. She explained that, not being able to follow them into the church with her donkey, she had decided to come where they found her and wait for them there.

"Does no one at all live here?" Lanfear asked, carelessly.

"Among the owls and the spectres? I would not pass

a night here for a lemonade! My mother," she went on, with a natural pride in the event, "was lost in the earthquake. They found her with me before her breast, and her arms stretched out keeping the stones away." She vividly dramatized the fact. "I was alive, but she was dead."

"Tell her," Miss Gerald said, "that my mother is dead, too."

"Ah, poor little thing!" the girl said, when the message was delivered, and she put her beast in motion, chattering gayly to Miss Gerald in the bond of their common orphanhood.

The return was down-hill, and they went back in half the time it had taken them to come. But even with this speed they were late, and the twilight was deepening when the last turn of their road brought them in sight of the new village. There a wild noise of cries for help burst upon the air, mixed with the shrill sound of maniac gibbering. They saw a boy running towards the town, and nearer them a man struggling with another, whom he had caught about the middle, and was dragging towards the side of the road where it dropped, hundreds of feet, into the gorge below.

The donkey-girl called out: "Oh, the madman! He is killing the signor!"

Lanfear shouted. The madman flung Gerald to the ground, and fled shrieking. Miss Gerald had leaped from her seat, and followed Lanfear as he ran forward to the prostrate form. She did not look at it, but within a few paces she clutched her hands in her hair, and screamed out: "Oh, my mother is killed!" and sank, as if sinking down into the earth, in a swoon.

"No, no; it's all right, Nannie! Look after her, Lanfear! I'm not hurt. I let myself go in that fellow's hands, and I fell softly. It was a good thing he didn't drop me over the edge." Gerald gathered himself up nimbly enough, and lent Lanfear his help with the girl. The situation explained itself, almost without his incoherent additions, to the effect that he had become anxious, and had started out with the boy for a guide, to meet them, and had met the lunatic, who suddenly attacked him. While he talked, Lanfear was feeling the girl's pulse, and now and then putting his ear to her heart. With a glance at her father: "You're bleeding, Mr. Gerald," he said.

"So I am," the old man answered, smiling, as he wiped a red stream from his face with his handkerchief. "But I am not hurt—"

"Better let me tie it up," Lanfear said, taking the handkerchief from him. He felt the unselfish quality in a man whom he had not always thought heroic, and he bound the gash above his forehead with a reverence mingling with his professional gentleness. The donkey-girl had not ceased to cry out and bless herself, but suddenly, as her care was needed in getting Miss Gerald back to the litter, she became a part of the silence in which the procession made its way slowly into Possana Nuova, Lanfear going on one side, and Mr. Gerald on the other to support his daughter in her place. There was a sort of muted outcry of the whole population awaiting them at the door of the locanda where they had halted before, and which now had the distinction of offering them shelter in a room especially devoted to the poor young lady, who still remained in her swoon.

When the landlord could prevail with his fellow-townsmen and townswomen to disperse in her interest, and had imposed silence upon his customers indoors, Lanfear began his vigil beside his patient in as great quiet as he could anywhere have had. Once during the evening the public physician of the district looked in, but he agreed with Lanfear that nothing was to be done which he was not doing in his greater experience of the case. From time to time Gerald had suggested sending for some San Remo physician in consultation. Lanfear had always approved, and then Gerald had not persisted. He was strongly excited, and anxious not so much for his daughter's recovery from her swoon, which he did not doubt, as for the effect upon her when she should have come to herself.

It was this which he wished to discuss, sitting fallen back into his chair, or walking up and down the room, with his head bound with a bloody handkerchief, and looking, with a sort of alien picturesqueness, like a kindly brigand.

Lanfear did not leave his place beside the bed where the girl lay, white and still as if dead. An inexpressible compassion for the poor man filled his heart. Whatever the event should be, it would be tragical for him. "Go to sleep, Mr. Gerald," he said. "Your waking can do no good. I will keep watch, and if need be, I'll call you. Try to make yourself easy on that couch."

"I shall not sleep," the old man answered. "How could I?" Nevertheless, he adjusted himself to the hard pillows of the lounge where he had been sitting and drowsed among them. He woke just before dawn with a start. "I thought she had come to, and knew everything! What a nightmare! Did I groan? Is there any change?"

Lanfear, sitting by the bed, in the light of the wasting candle, which threw a grotesque shadow of him on the wall, shook his head. After a moment he asked: "How long did you tell me her swoon had lasted after the accident to her mother?"

"I don't think she recovered consciousness for two days, and then she remembered nothing. What do you think are the chances of her remembering now?"

"I don't know. But there's a kind of psychopathic logic—If she lost her memory through one great shock, she might find it through another."

"Yes, yes!" the father said, rising and walking to and fro, in his anguish. "That was what I thought—what I was afraid of. If I could die myself, and save her from living through it—I don't know what I'm saying! But if—but if—if she could somehow be kept from it a little longer! But she can't, she can't! She must know it now when she wakes."

Lanfear had put up his hand, and taken the girl's slim wrist quietly between his thumb and finger, holding it so while her father talked on.

"I suppose it's been a sort of weakness—a sort of wickedness—in me to wish to keep it from her; but I *have* wished that, doctor; you must have seen it, and I can't deny it. We ought to bear what is sent us in this world, and if we escape we must pay for our escape. It has cost her half her being, I know it; but it hasn't cost her her reason, and I'm afraid for that, if she comes into her memory now. Still, you must do—But no one can do anything either to hinder or to help!"

He was talking in a husky undertone, and brokenly, incoherently. He made an appeal, which Lanfear seemed not to hear, where he remained immovable with his hand on the girl's pulse.

"Do you think I am to blame for wishing her never to know it, though without it she must remain deprived of one whole side of life? Do you think my wishing that can have had anything to do with keeping her—But this faint *may* pass and she may wake from it just as she has been. It is logical that she should remember; but is it certain that she will?"

A murmur, so very faint as to be almost no sound at all, came like a response from the girl's lips, and she all but imperceptibly stirred. Her father neither heard nor saw, but Lanfear started forward. He made a sudden clutch at the girl's wrist with the hand that had not left it and then remained motionless. "She will never remember now—here."

He fell on his knees beside the bed and began to sob. "Oh, my dearest! My poor girl! My love!" still keeping her wrist in his hand, and laying his head tenderly on her arm. Suddenly he started, with a shout: "The pulse!" and fell forward, crushing his ear against her heart, and listened with bursts of: "It's beating! She isn't dead! She's alive!" Then he lifted her in his arms, and it was in his embrace that she opened her eyes, and while she clung to him, entreated:

"My father! Where is he?"

A dread fell upon both the men, blighting the joy with which they welcomed her back to life. She took her father's head between her hands, and kissed his bruised face. "I thought you were dead; and I thought that mamma—" She stopped, and they waited breathless. "But that was long ago, wasn't it?"

"Yes," her father eagerly assented. "Very long ago."

"I remember," she sighed. "I thought that I was killed, too. Was it *all* a dream?" Her father and Lanfear looked at each other. Which should speak? "This is Doctor Lanfear, isn't it?" she asked, with a dim smile. "And I'm not dreaming now, am I?" He had released her from his arms, but she held his hand fast. "I know it is you, and papa; and yes, I remember everything. That terrible pain of forgetting is gone! It's beautiful! But did he hurt you badly, papa? I saw him, and I wanted to call to you. But mamma—"

However the change from the oblivion of the past had been operated, it had been mercifully wrought. As far as Lanfear could note it, in the rapture of the new revelation to her which it scarcely needed words to establish, the process was a gradual return from actual facts to the things of yesterday and then to the things of the day before, and so back to the tragedy in which she had been stricken. There was no sudden burst of remembrance, but a slow unveiling of the reality in which her spirit was mystically fortified against it. At times it seemed to him that the effect was accomplished in her by supernatural agencies such as, he remembered once somewhere reading, attend the souls of those lately dead, and explore their minds till every thought and deed of their earthly lives, from the last to the first, is revealed to them out of an inner memory which can never, any jot or tittle, perish. It was as if this had remained in her intact from the blow that shattered her outer remembrance. When the final, long-dreaded horror was reached, it was already a sorrow of the past, suffered and accepted with the resignation which is the close of grief, as of every other passion.

Love had come to her help in the time of her need, but not love alone helped her live back to the hour of that supreme experience and beyond it. In the absorbing interest of her own renascence, the shock, more than the injury which her father had undergone, was ignored, if not neglected. Lanfear had not, indeed, neglected it; but he could not help ignoring it in his happiness, as he remembered afterwards in the self-reproach which he would not let the girl share with him. Nothing, he realized, could have availed if everything had been done which he did not do; but it remained a pang with him that he had so dimly felt his duty to the gentle old man, even while he did it. Gerald lived to witness his daughter's perfect recovery of the self so long lost to her; he lived, with a joy more explicit than their own, to see her the wife of the man to whom she was dearer than love alone could have made her. He lived beyond that time, rejoicing, if it may be so said, in the fond memories of her mother which he had been so long forbidden by her affliction to recall. Then, after the spring of the Riviera had whitened into summer, and San Remo hid, as well as it could, its sunny glare behind its pines and palms, Gerald suffered one long afternoon through the heat till the breathless evening, and went early to bed. He had been full of plans for spending the rest of the summer at the little place in New England where his daughter knew that her mother lay. In the morning he did not wake.

"He gave his life that I might have mine!" she lamented in the first wild grief.

"No, don't say that, Nannie," her husband protested, calling her by the pet name which her father always used. "He is dead; but if we owe each other to his loss, it is because he was given, not because he gave himself."

"Oh, I know, I know!" she wailed. "But he would gladly have given himself for me."

That, perhaps, Lanfear could not have denied, and he had no wish to do so. He had a prescience of happiness for her which the future did not belie; and he divined that a woman must not be forbidden the extremes within which she means to rest her soul.